TERRAFIN

BATTLES THE
BOOM BROTHERS

Published by Puffin 2014
A Penguin Company
Penguin Books Ltd, 80 Strand, London, WC2R 0RL, UK
Penguin Group (USA) Inc., 375 Hudson Street, New York 10014, USA
Penguin Books Australia Ltd, 707 Collins Street, Melbourne, Victoria 3008,
Australia (A division of Pearson Australia Group Pty Ltd)
Canada, India, New Zealand, South Africa

Written by Cavan Scott
Illustrated by Dani Geremia – Beehive Illustration Agency

www.puffinbooks.com

ISBN: 978-1-40939-255-2
001
Printed in Great Britain

MIX
Paper from
responsible sources
FSC™ C018179

TERRAFIN

BATTLES THE
BOOM BROTHERS

by Onk Beakman

PUFFIN

CONTENTS

ABOUT THE AUTHOR

Onk Beakman knew he wanted to be a world-famous author from the moment he was hatched. In fact, the book-loving penguin was so keen that he wrote his first novel while still inside his egg (to this day, nobody is entirely sure where he got the tiny pencil and notebook from).

Growing up on the icy wastes of Skylands' Frozen Desert was difficult for a penguin who hated the cold. While his brothers plunged into the freezing waters, Onk could be found with his beak buried in a book and a pen clutched in his flippers.

Yet his life changed forever when a giant floating head appeared in the skies above the tundra. It was Kaos, attempting to melt the icecaps so he could get his grubby little hands on an ancient weapon buried beneath the snow.

Onk watched open-beaked as Spyro swept in and sent the evil Portal Master packing. From that day, Onk knew that he must chronicle the Skylanders' greatest adventures. He travelled the length and breadth of Skylands, collecting every tale he could find about Master Eon's brave champions.

Today, Onk writes from a shack on the beautiful sands of Blistering Beach with his two pet sea cucumbers.

CHAPTER ONE

PROFESSOR PUCK'S FANTASTIC FAIR

"**R**oll up, roll up! Professor Puck's Fantastic Fairy Fair is in town. You will be amazed! You will be astonished! You won't believe your eyes!"

Gurglefin the Gillman rubbed his webbed hands together with glee. He'd been waiting for this moment all year. Professor Puck's fair was famous throughout Skylands. Everyone knew about it. The crazy games, the fin-raising rides, the strange sights. And the delicious smells. Oh, the smells. Doughnuts, popcorn and pretzels, toffee apples, candyfloss and gingerbread. His mouth was watering at the very thought.

The only problem was what to try first. Everywhere he turned, Gurglefin was presented with fresh treats and new opportunities for fun and excitement. Lights flashed, music played and carnival folk called out, trying to entice him to their various stalls.

Then, something caught his eye. There, behind the helter-skelter and the Hook-a-Chompy, stood a small, modest looking red tent, with a hand-painted sign hung over its dark entrance.

MADAME DESTINY
FORTUNES TOLD,
FUTURES PREDICTED

"Yes," thought Gurglefin. "That's the place to start. Madame Destiny can tell me what I'd enjoy most."

He waddled over excitedly, coins ready to cross Madame Destiny's hand with silver. There

11

she was, hunched
over a crystal ball
in the mouth of
the tent. She
was wearing a
dark, crimson
scarf around
her head and a
pink, sequinned
veil across her
face. As he drew nearer,

Gurglefin slowed. There was something sinister
about the old woman. Something not quite
right. Maybe it was her piercing red eyes, or
the stubby fingers she waved over the crystal.

But, after coming this far, Gurglefin was in
no mood to be a scaredy-catfish. This was just
a harmless bit of fun, a harmless old woman.
Nothing to be afraid of at all.

He crept nearer the stall and cleared his
throat.

"Er, h-hello," he croaked. "Madame Destiny?"

The hag didn't look up. He tried again.

"Madame Destiny, I was wondering if you could –"

"What do you want?" the woman snapped, throwing her arms around the crystal as if trying to hide it from view.

"J-just to have my fortune told," stammered Gurglefin.

"And why should I do that?" she shrieked.

"Er, because you're a fortune-teller?" he suggested, holding out two coins in a shaking hand.

The old woman growled, looked at the coins and then looked at Gurglefin. Without warning, she shot out a hand, snaffled the coins away and snarled at the nervy Gillman.

"You want to know what the future holds?" she barked, fixing him with a wicked glare.

Gurglefin just nodded, wondering if he really did.

"Are you sure?" she teased, her veil shifting as if she was smiling underneath.

"I g-guess so . . ."

"Then I predict you will come to a STICKY END," Madame Destiny screamed. "NOW SLING YER HOOK, FISHFACE!"

Gurglefin did just that. He quickly scampered from the tent into the crowd, not looking back. Madame Destiny had been so cross, so angry. But why? And what did she mean? A sticky end? He didn't like the sound of that.

Gurglefin paused to catch his breath, gills flapping and heart racing. Perhaps coming to Professor Puck's Fantastic Fairy Fair hadn't been such a good idea after all.

Then he smelled something that made him all but forget his horrible experience with the fortune-teller.

"Candyfloss!"

Gurglefin followed his nose until he found a robot, producing stick after stick laden with wonderfully sweet-smelling candyfloss from a door in its chest.

"Hello sir," the robot chirped happily. "I am Floss-O-Tron 3000. Can I help you?"

"Candyfloss please," Gurglefin said eagerly, pressing a coin into the robot's outstretched metal hand.

"Certainly, sir," Floss-O-Tron said, handing over the biggest stick of candyfloss Gurglefin had ever seen. "You enjoy the rest of the fair."

"I will now," said Gurglefin, grabbing the stick and wandering happily away. Mmmmmmmm. This was the best candyfloss he'd ever tasted. It smelled fantastic, tasted even better and sounded like . . .

. . . hang on. It sounded like a clock. Since when did candyfloss tick?

No, Gurglefin realized with a start. It sounded like a bomb!

"Oh my Cod!" Gurglefin exclaimed, suddenly holding the treat at arm's length. "My candyfloss is going to explode!"

What was he saying? Of course it wasn't going to explode. It was candyfloss. Ticking candyfloss, yes, but sweets don't generally go bang in your face. Do they? Gurglefin laughed at his own panic. What a silly sardine he was.

Then he remembered Madame Destiny's words:

"You will come to a sticky end!"
Gurglefin screamed, and the candyfloss went
bang in his face.

CHAPTER TWO

"ROLL UP, ROLL UP!"

"**N**ow that's what I'm talking about!"

Terrafin the Dirt Shark punched the air as he appeared in the middle of Professor Puck's Fantastic Fairy Fair. Behind him, Sonic Boom and Hot Dog also flashed into existence, deposited in the middle of the field by one of Master Eon's magical Portals. Usually the sudden arrival of a walking shark, a griffin and a flaming lava hound would have drawn a crowd, but here they were just one wondrous sight among many. Not that Terrafin minded – like Gurglefin before him, the Dirt Shark had

18

been looking forward to this for a long time.

Terrafin – like his two companions – was a Skylander, a sworn protector of Skylands, a vast realm of floating islands and endless skies. Recruited by Eon, greatest of the Portal Masters, the Skylanders spent their days defending the vulnerable, fighting the forces of Darkness and generally being pretty amazing. But today was special. Today they were having a day off! The last few months had been bonkers. Their arch-enemy – the sinister Portal Master known as Kaos – had been trying to find an ancient artefact called the Mask of Power. Long ago, the Mask had been split into eight segments and scattered throughout Skylands, but now Kaos was trying to put it back together. He had one segment, but the Skylanders had found two others. No one really knew what would happen if Kaos completed the Mask, as the secrets of its true power had been lost in the mists of time. But they didn't want to find out. Kaos on his own was bad enough. Kaos with a super-duper mystical object from the dark times wasn't worth thinking about.

But for today, Terrafin didn't have to worry about evil Portal Masters, ancient magical artefacts or even the safety of Skylands. Today, all Terrafin and his Skylander buddies had to worry about was having fun with a capital F-U-N!

"Test your strength!" bellowed a voice nearby. "Make the bell ring and claim your prize!"

Terrafin's toothy grin spread even wider. Test your strength? No problem. He was so brawny that even his biceps had biceps. Flexing his muscles, the Dirt Shark hurried over to the strong man stall.

"Hey," Terrafin said, brandishing a gold coin. "I'd like a go!"

"Certainly sir," the dog-faced stallholder said, regarding the Skylander with shifty eyes. "If you could just wait your turn?"

In front of the Skylander, a tiny Mabu was

struggling to lift a massive, oversized hammer.

"That's it," the stallholder sneered. "Hit the target and ring that bell."

Hit the target? It was all the Mabu could do to pick up the hammer. Finally, with a grunt, the little fellow managed to swing the thing over his head. It thudded into the base of the Test Your Strength machine . . . but the bell didn't ring. In fact, the marker that was supposed to shoot up to the bell didn't even budge.

The stallholder sniggered at the disappointed Mabu.

"Never mind. Better luck next time."

"My turn," insisted Terrafin, flipping the coin at the stallholder and grabbing the hammer. He didn't like the way the stallholder had gloated. Not one bit.

Gritting his teeth, he swung the mallet and slammed it onto the target. BRRRING! The marker zoomed up the machine and clattered into the bell at the top, sending out an almighty

ringing sound.

"Oh yeah!" shouted the triumphant Terrafin. "I'm king of the ring. Now, give me my prize!"

Muttering congratulations, the stallholder reluctantly shoved a cuddly teddyclops into Terrafin's hands.

"Here ya go kid," Terrafin said, tossing the prize at the little Mabu before heading back to find his friends.

Across the way, Sonic Boom was enjoying a game of Hoop-a-Sheep with her chicks while Hot Dog was bouncing up and down on all fours.

"Hey Terrafin," the molten mutt barked excitedly. "Can we get some food now? Woof! Can we? Can we? Can we?"

But Terrafin didn't answer.

"You hear that, SB?" the shark asked, cocking his head to the side.

The griffin frowned. All she could hear was the sound of the fair – excited children, thundering rides and jaunty music. But wait, there was something else. Something quiet. Something sad.

"Someone's crying," she realized, her motherly instinct kicking in. "We need to find them."

"But I'm hungrrrrrrry," moaned Hot Dog.

"You're always hungry," snapped Terrafin, trying to work out where the sound was coming from. "Let's see what's wrong."

And with that they were off, Sonic Boom's chicks snapping back into their shells as their mother chased after Terrafin.

Hot Dog didn't follow though. Instead, he sat bolt upright, sniffing the air.

"Bow-wow-wow-wow," he yapped. "What's that?"

A smell had drifted over the fair; the sweetest, most mouth-wateringly delicious smell Hot Dog had smelled all day. Or at least, in the last five minutes. The pup glanced at his friends for a second and then bounded in the opposite direction, following his nose.

"It sounds like it's coming from just around this tent," Sonic Boom called over her shoulder. She had taken to the air to track down the weeping sound, her super-sensitive ears working overtime.

And she was right. Soaring around the tent, she came to rest beside a huge, slate-grey Stone Golem. The craggy creature was sat on the floor, hugging its moss-covered knees, its massive boulder-like shoulders heaving with every heavy sob.

"Hey, what gives?" Terrafin asked, running up beside Sonic Boom.

The Stone Golem looked up and wiped a tear from his dark eyes.

"Oh, it's n-nothing," he sniffed, granite cheeks flushing with embarrassment.

"It doesn't look like nothing to me," Sonic Boom said kindly, placing a comforting paw on the Stone Golem's shoulder. Her eyes fell down to the rusty metal ring that was fastened around his ankle. "What's your name?"

"R-Rocky," the Stone Golem stammered, "and I'm fine. Really I am. It's just that I'm about to go on stage and I get really nervous before a gig."

"You're putting on a show?" Terrafin asked, his eyes lighting up. "That's cool." Before he had become a Skylander, Terrafin had been a

boxing champ and he still missed the thrill of the ring from time to time.

"Not for me," Rocky admitted. "I hate performing. Always have. Look at me. I'm so nervous I'm sweating pebbles."

"Then why put yourself through the ringer?" Terrafin asked, crossing his thick arms across his broad chest. "Throw in the towel if you hate it so much."

"I can't," Rocky whimpered, his voice surprisingly small for such a large creature. "He won't let me."

"Who won't?" asked Sonic Boom and immediately got her answer.

"Rocky?" came a booming voice from behind them. "Where are you, you snivelling slag heap? If I find you crying again . . ."

At the very sound of the voice, Rocky crumbled, his tears flowing freely again.

"*He* won't," the Stone Golem whined. "Professor Puck."

Terrafin and Sonic Boom exchanged a worried glance. Rocky was obviously petrified of whoever was hollering. Not that they could blame him. Whoever it was, they sounded terrifying.

"Rocky!" the voice bellowed. "There you are . . ."

Gulping, Terrafin turned to see the owner of the deafening voice, expecting to find a huge giant looming over them. His eyes grew wide as he saw who the voice really belonged to.

28

CHAPTER THREE

THE PROFESSOR

Professor Puck wasn't a massive, muscle-bound mountain of a man. In fact, he hardly came up to Terrafin's knees. He was a gnome, and even by their titchy standards, a short one at that.

Dressed in red velvet tails and wearing a hat nearly as tall as he was, he bustled towards the amazed Skylanders.

"Rocky," he thundered, his voice impossibly loud for such a small fellow. "This is ridiculous. Do we have to go through this every time?"

"Hey, give the guy a break," Terrafin cut in. "Can't you see he's upset?"

Puck spun on his heels and fixed Terrafin with

a beady stare. "And who might you be?" he snapped, his admittedly impressive moustache twitching beneath a bulbous nose. "This area is out of bounds for the general public."

"Well it's a good job we're not the general public then," Terrafin growled, his fin flicking with frustration. "We're Skylanders."

Even that didn't seem to make any impact.

"Well, whoever you are, you are in Professor Puck's way. Stand aside, sir."

Dumbstruck, Terrafin did what he was told – something that didn't happen very often.

"Now, pull yourself together, Rocky m'boy," Puck barked. "It's show time!"

"But I don't want to," the Stone Golem snivelled, his head hanging low. "You know I go to pieces in front of an audience."

He wasn't joking. Rocky had been crying so hard that one of his shoulder boulders had rolled loose.

"Nonsense. You're the biggest rock star this

fair has ever known. Pull yourself together, lad. Your adoring public awaits."

Shrugging, Rocky started to gather himself together – literally. But Sonic Boom wasn't happy. She hated bullies, even the really small ones.

"Now listen here," she began, her bright eyes narrowing – but she was cut short by a sudden bark.

"Woof, woof!"

"That's Hot Dog," said Terrafin, forgetting about the teary golem for a second. Sure enough, the smouldering puppy came scampering around the corner and skidded to a halt.

"Terrafin," he panted, his hot breath misting in the air. "You gotta see this. Woof. Come quickly."

And with that he was gone, pelting back from where he came, leaving a trail of steaming paw prints in the mud.

Terrafin glanced at Rocky, torn between a rock and a hot hound.

"You gonna be OK, kid?" he asked. The Stone Golem nodded gravely.

"That's it," Puck said, clapping Rocky on the back (well, the back of his ankles at least). "The show must go on!"

Still uneasy about leaving the golem in the clutches of the menacing gnome, Terrafin and Sonic Boom took off after Hot Dog. They'd never seen the fiery pooch so frazzled. What on earth had he found?

"You'll never guess what I've found," Hot Dog yapped as they raced across the fair. Terrafin, while no slouch, had struggled to keep up with the puppy and so dived underground to swim after him. Like all Dirt Sharks, Terrafin could burrow through the earth at blistering speeds.

They raced by toffee-apple pie stands and Cyclops Mammoth Carousels, before Hot Dog skidded to a halt in front of what looked like a statue made out of candyfloss.

"Looks tasty," admitted Terrafin, licking his lips.

"Smells even better," agreed Hot Dog. Sonic Boom had to agree. Even her chicks were bouncing around in their shells at the sugary sweet smell. "I couldn't believe my luck when I found it, but look . . ."

Resting on his hind legs, Hot Dog leant against the pink fluffy statue and gave it a long, hard lick with a scalding tongue.

"Ow. Watch it, flame-features," came a voice from inside the statue. "That's hot!"

"Wait a minute," said Terrafin in amazement. "I know that voice."

Hot Dog had licked away some of the candyfloss to reveal a familiar fishy face.

"Gurglefin!" Sonic Boom exclaimed. "What are you doing in all that candyfloss?"

"Well, it's what every Gillman's wearing this season," Gurglefin sighed, rolling his big googly eyes.

"Really?" asked Hot Dog, looking puzzled.

Puppies never really followed the latest fashion trends.

"Of course not," Gurglefin spluttered. "For heaven's hake, I'm trapped. This is worse than the day I accidently sailed into the . . . the . . . Tartar Sauce Sea! GET ME OUT OF HERE!"

Now Hot Dog was grinning. The thought of slurping all that candyfloss was making his taste buds sizzle.

"No, no, no," Gurglefin quickly added. "Not you. You'll burn my scales off."

Hot Dog's face fell as Terrafin prodded the sticky stuff.

"I think it's drying out. I guess I could punch it off you."

"Wah!" wailed Gurglefin, wriggling within his personal pink prison. "Please don't. This is one fish that would prefer not to be battered!"

"Step aside boys," said Sonic Boom, taking a deep breath. "This needs a mother's touch."

"Or at least her voice," Terrafin warned,

realizing what was about to happen. "Cover your ears!"

"Wait, I can't," spluttered Gurglefin. "My arms are . . ."

It was too late. Sonic Boom opened her beak and yelled. Now all mums can yell, but not like Sonic Boom. Her screech can knock over trees and even dislodge mountains, so a pile of candyfloss was no problem. A tsunami of sonic shock waves washed over Gurglefin, ripping the sticky substance from his scales. In a few seconds he was clean of the stuff. He was also flat on his back, knocked flying by the force of

Sonic's vocal assault.

"Hey, you alright little fella?" asked Terrafin, scooping the Gillman back off the floor.

"Ask me when my ears have stopped ringing," Gurglefin spluttered. "Like in a hundred years."

"But who did this to you?" barked Hot Dog. "How did you get covered in candy?"

Shaking his head to try and clear his ears, Gurglefin told them about Floss-O-Tron 3000 and the ticking candyfloss.

"Candy that goes kaboom?" Terrafin said when Gurglefin had finished his fishy tale. "That sure ain't sweet."

"We need to warn Professor Puck about this," Sonic Boom insisted. "If one of his serving robots has malfunctioned someone could get hurt."

"Warn him?" growled Terrafin, slamming a fist into his open palm. "I bet that nasty little gnome is behind it. There's something not right about that Puck punk."

From her tent, Madame Destiny's eyes grew wide as she watched the three Skylanders storm across the fairground, with Gurglefin stumbling behind.

Skylanders? Here? That could ruin everything.

Quick as a flash, she hurried into their path, trying to stall them.

"Well, hello big boy," she cooed, fluttering her long eyelashes at Terrafin. "Cross my palm with silver and I'll tell you what the future holds."

"I know what it holds, sister," Terrafin snarled, barging past the fortune-teller. "A narky gnome is about to go three rounds with the champ."

Madame Destiny turned her attention to Sonic Boom. "What about you, my dear? Need to know what tomorrow brings?"

"Don't listen to her codswallop, Sonic Boom," sniffed Gurglefin, remembering their earlier encounter. "That lousy landlubber's a fake. A phoney."

"Is that right, fish-face?" Madame Destiny growled, her false smile faltering behind her sequin-covered veil. "Come back here and I'll give you a right grilling."

But the Skylanders were gone. Madame Destiny glowered after them, red eyes blazing with hatred. She scuttled back to her tent, tripping on her long gown, and disappeared inside.

There, in the shadows of the tent, a crystal ball sat on a velvet-covered table. As Madame Destiny approached the sphere it began to glow, responding to her presence. She raised her stubby hands, causing an eerie mist to swirl inside the globe, and muttered a magic spell under her breath. Slowly but surely, a face began to form in the glass, its big black eyes staring up at her from beyond.

"Ah, there you are," she hissed, her brow creased into a frown. "We've got a problem. There are Skylanders here. We need to move now, before they ruin everything."

She chuckled a chuckle that soon turned into a cackle, followed by a full-blown evil laugh.

"The fools are doomed, I tell you. DOOOMED!"

CHAPTER **FOUR**

ROCKY ROCKS OUT

Far away, in the Eternal Archive, home to every book ever written (and even a few that weren't), Sprocket the Tech Skylander was on her way to meet Eon. She had to admit she was getting worried about the Portal Master. He looked as if he hadn't slept for days. Actually, Sprocket didn't even know if Eon needed to sleep, but she knew she had never seen him looking so tired. And so old. It was this business with the Mask of Power. He had been working with the Eternal Archive's Warrior Librarians to track down the remaining segments of the Mask before Kaos could, but the strain was beginning to show. Eon had protected Skylands for centuries, but was it now becoming too much?

"Ah, there you are Sprocket," Eon said as she turned the corner. She tried not to stare at the dark rings under the old man's eyes. "We need to check in with Squirmgrub and see if the Book of Power has revealed the location of the next segment. I'm worried that we haven't heard from him."

Squirmgrub was the Warrior Librarian who had been assigned to watch over the fabled Book of Power, the magical tome that held the secrets of the Mask itself. There was something about the armoured archivist that Sprocket didn't trust, but now was not the time to raise her concerns. Keeping quiet, she followed Eon to the vault where the Book was kept – but when they got there they found the vault empty. The Book was there of course, magically bound to its lectern so no one could remove it, but where was Squirmgrub?

"This is most peculiar," Eon muttered, his staff tapping on the Vault's stone cold slabs. "He should be here."

"That's not all, Master Eon," Sprocket said, rushing over to the book. "Look." Pictures had formed on the Book's open pages. The magical images shifted and changed as Sprocket watched.

"It must be the location of the Earth segment," Eon said gravely. "But why didn't Squirmgrub report this?"

"And look where it is," prompted Sprocket. "Isn't that . . ."

"Professor Puck's Fantastic Fairy Fair," Eon uttered gravely. "Terrafin and the others have already gone there."

"Well, that's a spot of luck, then," Sprocket said cheerfully, before noticing that the picture was changing again. The image of the fair was blurring, to be replaced by a picture of a tall hulking figure.

"What is that?" she asked, as the lines came into focus.

"It looks like a Stone Golem to me," replied the Portal Master, running a wrinkled hand through his snowy-white beard.

"Ladies and Gentlemen, are you ready to rock and roll?" The spotlight swept across the large tent's stage, finally resting on the tiny figure of Professor Puck. The gnome was standing, arms thrown out wide – well, as wide as they could go – as he addressed the audience.

"Are you ready to dance like you've never danced before?"

The audience shouted yes, hundreds of eager faces all looking up expectantly.

"Then please welcome to the stage the next big thing, the ultimate rolling stone, the slab-faced singer with a voice that can move mountains. Give it up for the one, the only . . . ROCKY THE ROCKER!"

As one the crowd started to chant. "Rocky! Rocky! Rocky!"

"Woah, the place is packed," Terrafin commented as he ducked beneath the tent flaps. "Are these all Rocky's fans?"

"Sounds like it," said Sonic Boom, shoving her way in. "I didn't realize he was this popular."

"Oh, I can't stand crowds," moaned Gurglefin as he and Hot Dog entered. "Crammed in like a tin of sardines. But at least they aren't dancing."

"What's wrong with dancing?" Hot Dog woofed, his tail wagging with excitement. "I love to burn up the dance floor."

"I always floundered in dance class back at fish school," Gurglefin shrugged. "I've got two webbed feet."

"You've got no sole man," shouted Terrafin, struggling to be heard over the crowd's chanting. "But for now you're right. This is no time to shake our tail fins. We need to find Professor Puck."

"He's up there on stage," pointed out Sonic Boom. "And look – there's Rocky."

The crowd went mad as the Stone Golem appeared on the stage. They whooped and they hollered, even though Rocky was visibly shaking.

"He looks ruff," barked Hot Dog.

"Must be stage fright," said Terrafin. "I saw it all the time back in the ring. People freeze in the spotlight."

But Rocky didn't freeze. Despite his obvious nerves, the Stone Golem stepped up to the mic and cleared his throat.

"I guess any fin is possible," grumbled Gurglefin. "But Stone Golems aren't known for their singing. Their voices are just too gravelly."

A second later the Gillman was eating his

words. The Skylanders couldn't believe their ears when the golem began his song. He was brilliant. They had never heard someone sing so well. His voice wasn't rough. It was smooth and strong and so, so tuneful.

For a second, Terrafin forgot all about Floss-O-Tron 3000 and the exploding candyfloss and Professor Puck. His toes began to tap and his legs began to move. Before he knew what was happening he was dancing to the beat. Everyone was dancing. The crowd, Sonic Boom, Hot Dog . . . even Gurglefin. The Gillman was spinning on his back and flipping in the air.

"Hey, I thought you said you can't dance?" Terrafin said, as Gurglefin pulled off a perfect pirouette.

"I can't," the Gillman gasped. "I hate dancing. Really I do, but I just can't stop myself."

It was true. Terrafin suddenly realized that he couldn't stop dancing either. He tried to stand still but his feet kept stomping. Sonic Boom was

the same. Even the griffin's chicks were bouncing in and out of their shells in a riotous routine.

"W-what's happening?" cried out Gurglefin as he body-popped across the dance floor.

"It's Rocky's singing voice," realized Sonic Boom as she jived on the spot. "It must be magical."

"It's making us dance," barked Hot Dog, "and I love it. Woof. It's a disco inferno."

"Holy carp!" shouted Gurglefin, pointing up. "Your stony rock star isn't the only one up there. Look!"

Terrafin glanced around at the stage. There, lurking in the shadows, was a robotic figure.

"Perhaps that's his backing singer?" suggested Hot Dog.

"No it's not," insisted Gurglefin. "That's Floss-O-Tron 3000, and it looks to me like he's brewing a new batch of his popping candy!"

Sure enough, the door in the robot's chest was glowing a sickly pink colour. With an evil

grin on his polished
face, Floss-O-Tron
reached inside and
started pulling out
stick after stick of
candyfloss.

"Who wants some
candy?" the robot
cried and the crowd
cheered back, thinking
this was all part of
the show. Even Rocky
didn't seem fazed. Despite his nerves, he looked
lost in his music.

"We need to stop that robot," yelled Sonic
Boom.

"I'm trying," insisted Terrafin, "but I'm stuck
in the groove. I want to bust heads but I can't
stop busting a move."

None of them could. They could only watch as
the robot started flinging his ticking candyfloss

on to the dance floor. The Skylanders tried to warn the jigging crowd, but they couldn't hear anything over Rocky's voice. One by one, the hungry masses scooped up the candyfloss and started gobbling it down.

And then the first candy-grenade went boom.

SPLAT!

SPLAT!

SPLAT!

All over the tent the sweet-bombs went off, smothering everyone in the syrupy stuff. The crowd was covered, the Skylanders were covered, even Professor Puck was covered.

"I . . . can't . . . .. move . . ." Terrafin growled, struggling against the glistening gunk.

"Neither can I," barked Hot Dog, "but it tastes great."

"At least the music's stopped," said Gurglefin, breathing a sigh of relief. "Fintastic."

On the stage, Rocky had been shocked into silence and the spell was broken – not that it really mattered. No one could dance any more. They had all been transformed into solid, sugary statues.

"Didn't anyone ever tell you that too many sweets are bad for your health?" jeered Floss-O-Tron, before tugging aside the stage curtain. "Come on boys, grab the golem."

The Skylanders could only watch helplessly as trolls of all shapes and sizes streamed onto the stage. The green goblins rushed over to Rocky and pushed the helpless singer over onto his side.

"Leave him alone," Terrafin yelled, but it was no good. Sniggering, the trolls rolled the gloop-smothered golem off the stage and out to who-knows-where.

"Bye bye," Floss-O-Tron said as it disappeared after them. "Sweet dreams, Skylanders!"

CHAPTER FIVE

A STICKY SITUATION

"They've golem-napped Rocky," Professor Puck wailed from beneath a mountain of hardened candyfloss. "My number one star, nabbed from beneath my nose. The best money-spinner I've ever had, snatched away. SOMEBODY DO SOMETHING!"

"So, I guess Puck's not behind all this after all," shrugged Sonic Boom (which was extremely difficult to do, given that she couldn't move).

"Maybe, maybe not," rumbled Terrafin. "All I know is that we can't stick around here for much longer. Old stony face needs our help."

"But we're frozen in floss from head to flipper," spluttered Gurglefin, as Puck continued to moan. "What are we supposed to do? And can somebody please do something about Puck carping on? His whinging is reelly beginning to wear fin."

"Fin! Ha!" Hot Dog yapped. "You crack me up!"

"Crack me up?" shouted Terrafin, an idea occurring to him. "That's it. You need to crack me up!"

"You want more fish puns?" asked the confused Gillman. "This is hardly the time or plaice."

"No!" Terrafin yelled, cutting him off. "I don't mean like that. Hot Dog, we need your best firebark pronto. Burn me up."

"You want me to bark a fireball at you?" the pup replied, not quite believing what he was hearing.

"Not at me, at the candyfloss covering me. Can you do it?"

"Sure I can. One burning bow-wow-wow coming up."

Straining against his sweet restraints, Hot Dog barked, shooting a red-hot ball of flame at Terrafin. The fire sizzled over the shark's candy coating, causing Terrafin to suck air through his sharp teeth.

"OK," he hissed. "Getting hot under the collar here, but it's doing the trick."

As the flames subsided, the Skylanders realized what Hot Dog had done. The heat had toasted Terrafin's candyfloss, crystallizing it into a hard, pink shell.

"SB, it's your turn. Scream at me mama."

Sonic Boom smiled, catching Terrafin's drift. She opened her beak and roared at the Dirt Shark. Her ear-splitting screech shattered the hardened candy into a hundred glittering shards.

Terrafin was free.

"Oh, yeah," he grinned, flexing his aching muscles. "You're a knockout, SB. Now, you two free everyone else and I'll get after those thieving trolls. They won't know what's hit them."

With that, Terrafin jumped in the air, threw himself into a backflip and dived headfirst into the ground. As he burrowed away, Hot Dog was already preparing another fire ball.

"Woof woof. Who's next?" he asked, his eyes resting gleefully on Gurglefin.

"Just make sure you don't flame-grill me," the Gillman whimpered, screwing his eyes up tight.

Across the other side of the fair, Sprocket Portalled in. Eon had told her to meet with the other Skylanders and track down the Stone Golem. But where were they going to find a Stone Golem in the middle of a fun fair?

It was then she saw the troop of trolls rolling Rocky across the grass. OK, so maybe finding a Stone Golem in the middle of a fun fair wasn't so difficult after all.

With a cry of "The fix is in!" Sprocket tore
across the green, her armour's blasters buzzing
as they charged. Then she saw something out
of the corner of her eye. To her right, a couple
of Mace Major Trolls had grabbed a fortune-
teller and were pulling the poor soul towards a
giggling D. Riveter. The D. Riveter had already
raised its plasma rifle and was preparing to fire.

"Help me!" the woman shrieked, struggling

helplessly against her captors. "I predict this is going to get very nasty."

"Oh no you don't," Sprocket yelled, changing direction and racing towards the stricken fortune-teller. "I'm all tooled up."

As she ran, she gripped a massive metal wrench. Despite being a Golding, Sprocket had always preferred gadgets over gold. From an early age she had assisted her barmy old inventor of an uncle, tinkering with gizmos and doohickeys in his workshop. Now she used her tools to defend Skylands.

"Oh save me Skylander, save me," the fortune-teller cried as the Mace Majors yanked at her arms. They looked like they were trying to rip her limb from limb. "They're going to blast me into a million little pieces!"

"Not if I have anything to do with it." Sprocket raised the wrench above her head. "I'm built to . . . woah."

At the last moment the D. Riveter twisted,

its cannon coming round to face Sprocket. It squeezed the trigger, a bolt of brilliant blue light sizzling towards the Skylander. Sprocket swivelled just in time, swinging her wrench around. The energy bolt slammed into the supersized tool, and ricocheted back to blast the D. Riveter off its feet.

"Ha!" Sprocket shouted defiantly. "There's more where that came from!" In front of her, the air began to shimmer.

As a Tech Skylander, Sprocket could build defensive gun turrets out of nothing. Already the tower was clanking together, components and cogs sparking into view. "If I build it, it will shoot."

"Then we'd better stop you."

A pair of heavy metal arms clamped around Sprocket. Someone had grabbed her from behind and was pinning her arms to her side. Someone incredibly strong. She couldn't move. She turned her head, straining to see her attacker and found herself face-to-face with a grinning robot.

"Would you like some candyfloss?" it asked.

Terrafin couldn't believe his eyes when he burst out of the ground. What was Sprocket doing here? And why was she caught in Floss-O-Tron's cybernetic clutches?

And then there was that annoying fortune-teller, Madame Destiny, being tormented by a bunch of trolls. Who should he rescue first?

There was no contest really. Sprocket looked in trouble, but he knew she could handle herself. The first rule of being a Skylander is protecting the weak – and the fortune-teller sure looked scrawny.

"Yo, green nose. You've got a choice," Terrafin roared, clenching his fists and getting ready for a fighting frenzy. "Drop the dame or I'll drop you."

Amazingly, the trolls just laughed.

"Did you hear me? Don't make me come over there and body slam yo' face."

That seemed to do it. The Mace Majors let go of Madame Destiny's arms . . . but only to produce two huge maces from behind their horrible warty backs.

"So you wanna go toe-to-toe with the champ, do you?" Terrafin said, now spoiling for a punch up. He raised his fists, metal spikes bursting across his knuckles. "Then let's go, fools."

"You see, that's the thing," said Madame Destiny, who hadn't moved an inch from where the trolls had released her. "I don't think they're the fools at all. The only foolish fool I can see is you, SKYBLUNDERER!"

Madame Destiny reached up with a ring-covered hand and ripped the veil from her face. Terrafin's jaw dropped open in amazement. "Woah," he said. "I did NOT see that coming."

Madame Destiny wasn't a fortune-teller at all. She wasn't even a lady.

Madame Destiny was Kaos.

"What are you waiting for, IDIOTS?" the evil Portal Master screeched. "ATTAAAAACK!"

The Mace Majors didn't wait to be told twice. They charged forward, maces held high. As Sprocket struggled against the vice-like grip of the souped-up serving robot, Terrafin dodged the first mace, but was whacked around the fin by the second. Seeing stars, he twisted and his fist connected with one Mace Major's jaw. The troll was launched into the air, arching towards Kaos. The Portal Master managed to step out of the way before being flattened, but caught one of his high-heels in the hem of his frock and ended up on his rear anyway.

"FOOOLS! Finish the SKYLOSER off!" the Portal Master yelled as he struggled back to his feet.

Terrafin threw himself back, narrowly missing another mace, and punched out, knocking the other Mace Major flying. But the fight was far from over. Terrafin gasped in pain as plasma bolts slammed into his dorsal fin. The D. Riveter had him in its sights.

"Lord Kaos, what shall we do with the golem?" said a voice, as another troll ran up to the wicked Portal Master's side. It was Glumshanks, Kaos' henchman, butler and general dogsbody. Behind him, Rocky was being rolled over and over. "It's just that the candyfloss is starting to weaken. If he breaks free . . ."

"Don't fuss, Glumshanks," shouted Kaos, clicking his fingers. In a flash, Madame Destiny's tent was replaced by a Portal of Power. "Just get him on the Portal. Must I think of everything?"

"You can think about how you'll feel when I bellyflop you," called Terrafin as he burrowed under the ground and burst from beneath the D. Riveter's feet, knocking the troll senseless. "Now release Sprocket and give up the golem."

"And I suppose you're going to stop me,

Terraflop?" the Portal Master jeered. "You and whose army?"

"Well, there's me for a start," yapped a voice from behind. Kaos whirled round to see Hot Dog flaming towards him.

"And don't forget us," added Sonic Boom, as her clutch of terrible toddlers burst from their eggs to glare at the goggling Portal Master.

Even Gurglefin got in on the act. "And just in case you were wondering," he said, dropping into a highly-impractical martial arts position, "I'm a black belt in Jellyfish Jujitsu. Hiiiii-yah!"

"Oh no," Kaos wailed. "Not three Skylanders and a karate-chopping Gillman. I'm doooooomed."

And then the Portal Master started to giggle.

"Yeah, laugh it up baldy," said Terrafin, stalking forwards. "You'll be sniggering on the other side of yo' face when Sprocket breaks free from your crazy candyfloss seller."

"Yes, because she's doing so well with

that," sniggered Kaos, wiping a tear from his eye. "Those arms are fitted with the toughest hydraulic muscles this side of the Junkyard Isles. She'll never break free."

"And you'll never take Rocky," Sonic Boom insisted, throwing her wings out wide.

"Wrong again, bird brain," Kaos crowed. "Floss-O-Tron, initiate the sequence of certain self-destruction – with added BOOOOOM!"

"Initiating," Floss-O-Tron replied, clicking his head around sharply. Immediately, brilliant pink light spilled out from behind Sprocket as the robot's engines roared and its gears spun.

"Listen to the sounds of your destruction, DIMWITS," Kaos cawed. "Flossy here has gone into overdrive. When he blows, the entire fair will be smothered in suffocating candyfloss and your techy little chum will be at the centre of the blast. You're all doomed, doomed and TRIPLE-DOOOOOOOMED!!"

CHAPTER SIX

AN EXPLOSIVE SITUATION

Steam was pouring from Floss-O-Tron's ears, mouth and, weirdly, eyebrows.

"It won't let go," Sprocket shouted, as Kaos hitched up his dress and started towards the Portal of Power.

"Woof! What about Rocky?" Hot Dog yapped. The trolls had already loaded the stricken Stone Golem onto the Portal. "They're getting away."

"We'll deal with that later," yelled Terrafin. "We've got to stop this thing before it blows."

"So long, FOOOLS!" cawed Kaos from the

Portal. "I've enjoyed beating you. AGAIN!"

He clapped his hands and vanished in a flash of light, followed by Glumshanks, the trolls and the wailing Rocky.

Terrafin didn't notice. He was too busy trying to yank Floss-O-Tron's arms from around Sprocket.

"It's no use," the Golding said. "They won't budge. You'll have to rewire the robot. Stop it from self-destructing."

"Me?" Terrafin asked, his fin falling. "But I'm no good with Tech stuff."

"Well, I can't do it myself," Sprocket insisted. "I'm in a bit of a tight spot."

"And neither me nor Hot Dog have fingers," Sonic Boom added. "Unless you think we can blast it to pieces."

"Kaos has cast some pretty tricky Tech spells on this thing," Sprocket said. "It'll just explode. Quick, Terrafin, there should be an access panel on its back."

Grumbling, Terrafin ran behind the shuddering

robot and, finding the hatch, ripped the door off its hinges with his bare hands. He was greeted with a mess of colourful wires and cables.

"I don't even know where to begin."

"Look for a red wire with yellow stripes," Sprocket ordered. "Or is it a yellow wire with red stripes?"

"Make up your mind," Terrafin snapped, as the whirring noise coming from Floss-O-Tron grew ever-louder.

"Red wire with yellow stripes – definitely," she said, sounding more confident this time. "Pull it out and then replace it with the blue wire with green dots."

Terrafin tried to get his hands into the tangle of wires. The robot was now beginning to shake violently.

"It's no good. These fists were made for throwing punches, not rewiring overheating tin cans. My fingers are too big."

"Y-you're not suggesting I do it," gulped

Gurglefin. "I trout I'd do any better. There's got to be salmon else who could have a go?"

"Don't worry, 'Fin," Terrafin growled. "I know what to do. SB and Hot Dog, grab Sprocket's legs."

"Woah, wait a minute," Sprocket said as she felt a beak and a set of red-hot-teeth clamp around her ankles. "There's no need to be hasty. If I can wriggle free, I could build a gun-o-matic and . . ."

"No time," interrupted Terrafin, appearing in front of her. Sprocket didn't like the way he was bunching his brass knuckles. "Just keep still. You won't feel a thing."

Sprocket screwed her eyes up tight behind her goggles. Terrafin's steely gaze swivelled up to fix on the steaming robot. "As for you . . ."

WHACK!

It all happened so quickly. Terrafin sent a pile-driving uppercut smashing into the robot's chrome-plated chin. Floss-O-Tron shot into the air, but his arms were still wrapped around Sprocket who in turn was being anchored to the ground by Sonic Boom and Hot Dog.

With a screech of ripping metal, the arms tore from the robot's body and Sprocket fell back to the grass. Floss-O-Tron, meanwhile, rocketed into the sky like a firework just as its self-destruct sequence completed.

KA-BOOOOOOM!

The thunderous explosion echoed through the fun fair. High above the ground, Floss-O-Tron detonated, sending burnt candyfloss spraying out left, right and centre.

"Woah, that was close," sighed Terrafin as crispy flakes of pink sugar floated down like snow. "That was one robot who seriously punched above his weight."

"I'm never eating candyfloss again," said Sonic Boom, helping Sprocket back to her feet.

"The same can't be said for everyone," the Golding laughed as Hot Dog scampered around

catching the flakes on his tongue.

"But what about Kaos?" asked Gurglefin. "And the trolls?"

"And my number one star!" roared another voice. Professor Puck raced up as quickly as his stubby little gnome legs would carry him. The showman looked a real state. His once proud moustache was matted with stale sugar. "You must rescue Rocky!"

"What? So you can make more money from him?" snarled Terrafin, looming over the gnome. "What's the deal anyhow? Where did you find him?"

For the first time since they'd met, Puck actually looked sheepish. That's what happens when you're surrounded by four Skylanders. Four *angry* Skylanders.

"I found him on an expedition to the Ragged Ranges. I was looking for new animals to show at the fair and heard a remarkable voice. I started to dance . . . we all did . . . and I knew

I had to have whoever was singing."

Sonic Boom took a step forward, her wings folded back in fury. "So you just took him." The griffin had spent years in the mountains – the only place high enough to safely lay her eggs – and had known many Stone Golems of old. Despite their size and fearsome appearance, they were gentle giants; loners who hated crowds, preferring their own company. "We saw the ring around his leg. You chained him up and dragged him back to your fair."

"Just to make some dough," Terrafin growled. "I should whack you into next week for what you've done to that guy."

"S-s-so, you won't help me?" Puck stammered, wringing his hat in his podgy hands. "You won't find Rocky?"

"Oh, we'll find him all right," Terrafin promised, jabbing a thick finger into the Prof's chest. "But not for you."

"We'll do it for Rocky," Sonic Boom said, her

beak curled into a snarl.

"But where do we start?" Hot Dog yapped, his belly finally full. "We don't know where Kaos has taken him."

"Perhaps we do," said Gurglefin picking up one of the hundreds of wooden candyfloss sticks that had tumbled down from the sky. The Gillman turned it over to show the Skylanders the name that was printed on its charred side.

"The Boom Brothers' Explosive Emporium," he read. "I know I'm no brain sturgeon, but maybe that's as good a place as any to start looking."

CHAPTER SEVEN

SQUIRMGRUB

"The Boom Brothers?" said Eon as he and Terrafin strode into the Eternal Archive's massive library. "I'm sure I've heard of them."

"Well, they're gonna hear about me when we track them down," growled Terrafin. "Who makes exploding candyfloss anyway?"

Eon strode down the main isle, bookshelves the size of giant cliffs rising up on each side. "Let's find out. The Encyclopaedia Skylandia is bound to have the information we seek."

The Encyclopaedia Skylandia is, as the name suggests, a set of encyclopaedias. It contains everything you need to know about Skylands – and a few things you don't need to know as well. Best of all is that it's enchanted. As new facts are discovered, new entries appear as if by magic on its pages. Sometimes entire new volumes pop into existence overnight.

For example, a few years ago, eminent Skylands historian Professor P. Grungally discovered that the monstrous fish that terrorizes Leviathan Lagoon has exactly 1,672½ teeth. How did he discover it? Well, the creature swallowed him during a fishing trip, but that's not important right now. The point is that even before Grungally managed to escape the beast's belly, the Leviathan entry in the Encyclopaedia Skylandia had already updated to include his discovery. No one knows how it works – it just does.

"If anything can help us find the Boom Brothers it's the Encyclopaedia," Eon insisted, tapping his staff against the floortiles as he scoured the shelves for the right volume. "It must be here somewhere."

"Er, can I help you?" came a voice from behind. Terrafin groaned. Squirmgrub the Warrior Librarian was rushing up behind them, mechanical arms flapping in the air. Master Eon insisted the armour-clad archivist was helping but, like Sprocket, there was something about Squirmgrub that Terrafin didn't like. There was just something . . . shifty about him.

Eon, however, was always willing to give people the benefit of the doubt.

"Ah, Squirmgrub," the Portal Master said, greeting the Librarian with a welcoming smile. "We're looking for information about The Boom Brothers' Explosive Emporium. I thought the Encyclopaedia might be able to help us."

For a brief moment, Terrafin thought he noticed the Librarian recognize the Boom Brothers' name.

"Maybe," Squirmgrub said. "Maybe not. I tell you what, there's no point you wading through all these dusty books. Why don't I look it up for you and let you know how I get on?"

"No can do," Terrafin cut in. "Kaos and his crazy cats have snatched Rocky. We need to get him back A.S.A.P."

"If not sooner," Eon added. "I believe Rocky has something to do with the Earth segment."

"Golly," Squirmgrub blustered, crossing, then uncrossing and then crossing his mechanical arms again. "The Earth segment. That is interesting. OK, let's have a look shall we?"

He bustled past, his telescopic eyes scanning the bookshelves. "I think we'll need volume 854. It should be up here somewhere."

"Between volumes 853 and 855?" Terrafin asked impatiently. He just couldn't bring himself to trust this guy.

Squirmgrub laughed, a high-pitched nervous titter. "Yes, exactly. Well done Terrabin."

"Terra*fin*," the Dirt Shark corrected with a snarl.

"Sorry, yes, that's what I meant." The Warrior

Librarian put his hands on his hips. "Oh dear. Deary, deary me. That is a shame."

"What is?" asked Eon, frowning.

"Volume 854 seems to be missing. Look." Squirmgrub pointed to a gap in the shelf between volumes 853 and 855. "That is most irregular. I will have to report it to the chief curator. Yes, I will have to do that straight away. Sorry I couldn't help you. Shall we go?"

But Eon didn't move. He was just standing there, staring at the gap where the book should be. "How disappointing. Especially as it's the very volume we're after. It's almost as if someone's removed it on purpose."

Terrafin was sure that the colour drained from the robot's paintwork.

"R-r-removed it on purpose? Oh, I doubt that, Master Eon. No Warrior Librarian would dream of doing such a thing."

"I'm pleased to hear it. But it doesn't matter. The Encyclopaedia Skylandia automatically updates. All we need to do is look up Volume 854 under 'V' . . ."

"And it'll tell us who stole it!" cut in Terrafin. "Hey, that's kinda smart."

"I'm a kinda smart kinda guy," said Eon with a wry smile as he ran a finger along the shelf. "Now, any idea where I'd find 'V', Squirmgrub?"

"Er, well, I-I-I'm not exactly sure . . ." stammered the Warrior Librarian, wringing his robotic hands together. "I could always check but . . . Oh, look!"

Eon turned, fixing the robot with a steely gaze. "Have you found something?"

The Warrior Librarian plucked a book off the shelf. "It's volume 854," he announced. "Someone must have put it in the wrong place."

"How careless of them," Eon said, holding out a hand. "But well done, Squirmgrub. May I have it?"

"Are you sure you don't want me to find what you're looking for?"

"No, I'm sure we can manage. You don't mind if we take it back to the other Skylanders, do you?"

"Well . . ." Squirmgrub hesitated before finally handing over the old leather-bound book. "No, I'm sure that would be fine."

"Thank you," Eon said graciously, tucking the volume under his arm. "Come on, Terrafin. Sonic Boom, Hot Dog and Sprocket will be waiting."

As they walked around the corner, leaving Squirmgrub in the aisle, Terrafin leant in close to the Portal Master.

"That was weird, Master Eon. It's almost like Squirmgrub was –"

"– hiding the book, yes." A shadow passed over the Portal Master's lined face. "But I'm sure it was an honest mistake . . ."

In the Encyclopaedia aisle, Squirmgrub waited until he was sure that Eon and Terrafin were gone before pressing a button on his wrist. With a hiss of hydraulics, a secret compartment opened on his robotic arm, revealing a small sphere – like a miniature crystal ball.

Squirmgrub lifted the sphere up to his mouth and whispered into it urgently. "Lord Kaos, can you hear me? The Skylanders know about the Boom Brothers. They're on their way . . ."

CHAPTER EIGHT

JUNK MOUNTAIN

Squirmgrub was right – the Skylanders were on their way. According to the Encyclopaedia Skylandia, the Boom Brothers were a pair of robots who specialized in explosions. Really big explosions. No one had ever seen them, although their factory – the legendary Explosive Emporium – was located in the Junk Mountains.

And, as Terrafin was about to find out, the Junk Mountains aren't exactly a beauty spot.

"Woah," the Dirt Shark said as Eon's Portal delivered them onto the side of one of the mountains. "This place is ugly with a capital UG."

"What are you talking about?" Sprocket gasped, a huge smile spreading across her face. "It's amazing!"

Hot Dog and Sonic Boom didn't say anything. They were just staring open-mouthed (or, in Sonic's case, open-beaked).

The Junk Mountains stretched as far as the eye could see, huge majestic peaks jutting into a hard, grey sky. But these weren't mountains of rock or even ice. They were mountains of rubbish. Everywhere the group looked were broken machines, clapped-out contraptions and mangled thingamabobs.

Instead of trees there were old twisted aerials and instead of bushes, heaps of tangled cables.

To Sprocket it looked like heaven. She was itching to dive in and see what she could build from all the discarded gadgets; what amazing inventions could be cobbled together from the piles of wrecked widgets.

But now wasn't the time. They had a job to do.

"So which way?" barked Hot Dog, scrambling up a crag of smashed-up stuff.

"The Encyclopaedia said the Explosive Emporium was at the top of the tallest mountain," remembered Terrafin. "So I guess we're climbing."

"Let me look," said Sonic, spreading her powerful wings and taking to the chilly air. The Skylanders watched as she shot up the side of the slope.

"I can see it," she shouted down. "Jutting out of the summit. A gigantic tower."

Terrafin peered upwards. Yes, he could see it too, rising into the sky high above them. Its walls were bright red and looked like metal glinting in the harsh sun. It resembled a huge rocket, supported on one side by what appeared to be some extremely rickety scaffolding.

"That's a long way up," Terrafin said, wondering if he could burrow his way to the summit. He tested the scrap-covered ground with his toe. Hmmm. Maybe not. He didn't want the giant mounds of twisted machines to crumble beneath their feet. "We better start climbing."

"I'll fly ahead to see if there are any –"

Sonic Boom didn't finish her sentence. A bashed-up oil barrel tumbled out of the sky and smacked her right between the eyes. The griffin let out a shocked screech and plunged down, stunned by the blow. Terrafin leapt up, caught her in his strong arms and somersaulted over, crashing back to the side of the mountain.

"You OK, SB?" he asked as the griffin shook her aching head.

"I was surprised, that's all," she replied, before her eyes widened. "Terrafin, look out! Above us!"

The Dirt Shark glanced up to see the remains of a rusty robot roaring down the mountain towards them. He threw up an arm to protect them, but Sonic was way ahead of him. A quick blast of shock waves smashed the wreckage into a thousand pieces, but they weren't out of danger just yet.

It was raining rubbish. Clumps of dented metal and battered machine parts were crashing down from above.

"What's going on?" woofed Hot Dog as he jumped to the side to avoid a plummeting kitchen sink.

"It's almost like someone is chucking junk down at us," yelled Sprocket, as a cracked toilet whistled by.

"Someone is!" growled Terrafin as a face loomed into view above them. A huge, ugly face. A huge, ugly, angry-looking face. A huge, ugly, angry-looking face made up of twisted, worn metal.

"RAAAAGH!" the monster bellowed, before throwing another fistful of busted machinery towards the Skylanders.

"It's a Trash Ogre!" shouted Terrafin,

punching the debris out of the way. "And it's trying to knock us off the side of the mountain!"

CHAPTER NINE

THE TRASH OGRE

A barrage of bashed-up machinery bounced down the mountain. No sooner had the Skylanders blasted it away, than the ogre's four arms would snatch up more junk, ready to hurl it at them.

And its aim was getting better! They wouldn't last much longer.

"Cover me," Sprocket said, leaping forward. "It's building time!"

As the other Skylanders punched, screeched and coughed up firebarks, Sprocket went to work, her arms moving so fast they began to blur. She grabbed this broken gizmo and that, fashioning them into a wall of garbage. In a flash, she was finished and stepped back to examine her handiwork.

"You've built a shield!" exclaimed Hot Dog happily, his tail wagging so fast it looked in danger of coming off.

"A rampart of rubbish," she announced, looking thoroughly pleased with herself until there was a large crash from the other side. "But it won't hold for long. How are we going to get past that ogre?"

"Perhaps we can get him to come past us," said Sonic Boom, a smile playing over her beak. "Sprocket, can you reinforce your barrier? Make it as strong as possible?"

Sprocket adjusted her goggles. "Of course I can."

"Then do it," Sonic said. "Terrafin, Hot Dog, can you help her?"

"Sure thing," said Terrafin. "But what are you

going to do, SB?"

"Give our ogre friend a taste of his own medicine."

With that, Sonic Boom beat her wings and flew up from behind Sprocket's shield.

As soon as the Trash Ogre spotted Sonic, it started flinging rubbish at her. She threw herself into a spiral to avoid the falling junk, and soared higher and higher. Sonic shot over the monster's misshapen head and climbed towards a ledge high above. Hoping that she'd given Sprocket enough time to reinforce the shield, she opened her beak and screamed at the top of her lungs.

Now, the top of Sonic Boom's lungs is a very high place indeed. A beam of pure sound waves slammed into the side of the mountain, but the griffin wasn't finished yet. She pulled back, looping around for another pass and let out another screech.

Beneath her, the ogre stopped throwing rubbish and scratched its head. Why was the griffin attacking the mountain? What had the mountain ever done to her?

Then the ogre heard a worrying rumble. Its mouth went dry and its metallic heart sank as it realized what she was trying to do. Above his head, the side of the mountain was moving, piles of junk tumbling down towards him.

Sonic Boom had set off an avalanche of rubbish!

The Trash Ogre didn't have time to react. With an ear-splitting roar, the wave of broken machines flooded over the monster, knocking it from its large flat feet. As Sonic hovered in the air like a hawk, the ogre was sent crashing down the side of the mountain. With a thud, it bounced off Sprocket's shield and tumbled all the way to the valley, several miles below.

The noise of the avalanche was deafening, even by Sonic Boom's standards. When it had passed, an eerie silence fell over the mountain range. The griffin's eyes narrowed. It was too

quiet. Had her friends survived the avalanche? Or had they been washed down the side of the mountain along with the ogre? Sonic swooped down, trying not to notice how much of a beating Sprocket's makeshift barrier had taken.

What if she'd got it wrong? What if she'd sent her fellow Skylanders to their doom?

"Way to go, SB!" yelled Terrafin happily as Sonic landed beneath the barrier. "You had that joker on the ropes! He's out for the count!"

Sprocket gave Sonic Boom a cheery thumbs up while Hog Dog bounded over and licked the griffin's cheek.

"Hey, hot stuff," she laughed. "Don't fry my feathers. Besides, it's not over yet. We've still got to climb to the top of the mountain."

"Yeah," agreed Terrafin, his grin turning grim. "And bust into the Explosive Emporium!"

CHAPTER TEN

THE EXPLOSIVE EMPORIUM

"Why can't people build their mountain-top lairs at the bottom?" grumbled Terrafin as they finally reached the summit. They had been climbing for hours and were frozen to the bone.

Well, at least three of them were.

"Come on slow coach," yapped Hot Dog as he scampered by. The combustible canine hadn't even broken into a sweat.

With a beat of her wings, Sonic Boom came to rest beside Terrafin and looked up at the scarlet tower that loomed menacingly over them.

The Explosive Emporium.

"So what's the plan?"

Terrafin considered this for a moment. "Tell you what. Why don't we batter our way in, kick troll butt, rescue Rocky, knock Kaos into the next dimension and then think of a plan?"

"Sounds good to me," beamed Sonic. "There's only one problem I can see."

"What's that?"

"That huge cannon."

Terrafin followed Sonic's gaze and groaned as he saw the massive gun that had appeared from a hatch in the side of the tower. The massive gun that was swivelling to target them.

"Take cover!" Terrafin yelled as the cannon opened fire. Mortars slammed into the rubbish at their feet, exploding on impact and sending them flying into the air. Terrafin found himself shooting over the side of the mountain and tumbling into free-fall before he felt Sonic Boom's claws close around his feet. By the time she had flown them back up to the summit, Sprocket had built a gun-o-matic and was returning fire while Hot Dog was summoning walls of fire to block the attack.

"We need to take out that gun," gasped Sonic Boom as a shot whistled by her ear, but Terrafin shook his head.

"No, SB. We need to take out the joker who's firing it. Dive burrow!"

Terrafin threw himself into the air, flipped

over a passing missile and then slammed back into the ground. Ow.

Burrowing through rusty metal was a lot harder than burrowing through earth, but he had to keep going. He'd tunnel beneath the tower walls, burst up on the other side and wallop the troll operating the gun. Easy!

Or so he thought.

KLAAAAAANG!

Under the ground Terrafin rubbed his aching head. He'd ploughed straight into something – something very hard. Reaching out, he knocked his brass knuckles against the metal wall that plunged beneath the surface. Who builds walls underground? Oh well. He'd just have to burrow harder.

Turning on his tail, Terrafin burrowed back to where his fellow Skylanders were still battling the giant cannon. But instead of breaking the surface, he started tunnelling round and round in circles, picking up speed, his fin flattening down as he swung back to rip towards the tower walls. Preparing for impact, he closed his eyes, clenched his jaw and . . .

CRASH!

Terrafin was through. With a shout of triumph, he threw himself up and burst from the floor. He'd picked up so much speed that he didn't stop, smashing through the tower and appearing behind the troll operating the cannon. The Mace Major twisted in his seat, his eyes wide with surprise. The last thing he expected to see was one of

Terrafin's massive shark-fists rushing towards him.

In fact it *was* the last thing he saw. The punch knocked the troll out stone cold.

There was only one problem. The cannon was still firing. It must have been switched to automatic. Frantically, Terrafin started thumbing buttons and flicking switches but it was no good. In fact, the cannon fired even more mortar shells at his friends.

Which was the right control? Which button would turn the thing off? With a grunt of exasperation, Terrafin did the only thing he could . . . and smashed his fist into the control panel.

There was a loud crack and a shower of sparks, and finally the gun fell silent.

Terrafin threw open a window and, seconds later, Sonic Boom swooped into the room, Hot Dog and Sprocket dangling from her claws. They were in! Now they just needed to find Rocky.

CHAPTER ELEVEN

INSIDE THE FACTORY

"So," said Sprocket. "Where next?"

"I wish I knew," admitted Terrafin, "but I'm open to ideas. This place is massive."

Sonic Boom was about to reply when she noticed Hot Dog. The fiery pooch was sniffing around in the corridor outside the cannon room.

"Hot Dog?" she asked. "What have you found, boy?"

The pup barked excitedly, embers flicking off his tail as it wagged. "Ruff ruff. Rocky's been this way. Look."

Terrafin peered closer. Hot Dog was nudging

a pile of tiny, smooth pebbles with his steaming nose.

"Hey, I've seen those before," he realized.

"They're the pebbles Rocky sweats when he's nervous," remembered Sonic Boom.

"And there's more," barked Hot Dog as he bounded down the corridor, his internal fire lighting up the dark passage. "Woof. Lots more."

"That's brilliant, Hot Dog," Sonic Boom praised as the Fire Skylander beamed with pride. "If we follow the pebbles . . ."

"We'll find Rocky!" cheered Terrafin.

The Skylanders crept through the Boom Brothers' factory, following the trail of pebbles. All around, in massive workshops, robots and trolls were making weird and not so wonderful weapons. There were bombs in all shapes and sizes. Bombs that looked like hamburgers. Bombs that looked like mushrooms. Bombs that looked like clocks and books and treasure chests and

sheep. There were even bombs that looked like sheep sitting on treasure chests, reading books while checking the time and eating mushroom-filled hamburgers (which, admittedly, did look a bit daft). There were robots fitting fuses here, robots setting timers there and trolls packing explosives into crates everywhere.

The Skylanders were almost seen a couple of times but managed to hide behind packing crates or piles of exploding yo-yos. They climbed higher and higher, sneaking up ladders and darting through doorways when no one was looking. And all the time the factory echoed to the sound of announcements being made over the loud speakers.

"Attention all workers," blared a speaker above Terrafin's head. "This is Boom One."

The Dirt Shark shared a look with Sonic Boom. That must have been one of the Boom Brothers.

"And Boom Two too," snapped an irritated

voice. The other explosive-loving sibling?

"Yes, yes, they know that," said Boom One, sounding more than a little peeved. "Can't you let me do anything by myself?"

"Not if I want it done right."

There was an irritated pause and then Boom One addressed the workers again.

"The next shift will commence in ten minutes. I repeat, ten minutes."

"No, you jumped up toaster," cut in Boom Two. "The shift starts in five minutes."

"Ten minutes!"

"Five minutes!"

"TEN MINUTES YOU STUPID BUCKET OF –"

KLANG! There was the sound of something metal being whacked by a spanner and Boom One said "Ow", before sheepishly announcing: "Next shift starts in five minutes. Thank you."

"So, *that's* the infamous Boom Brothers," said Sonic Boom, shaking her head.

"Sounds like they have trouble getting along,"

observed Sprocket.

"Do you think they'll have any food? Ruff ruff!" asked Hot Dog hopefully.

Terrafin gave Hot Dog a sharp look and pointed ahead of them. "Look, the trail of pebbles ends by those big red doors. I bet they've got Rocky in there."

"Then what are we waiting for?" barked Hot Dog. "Let's go!"

He was about to scamper over to the doors when Sprocket grabbed his collar.

"No, wait," she hissed as four Grenade General trolls pushed a trolley of explosives down the corridor. "We'll be spotted."

"Oh no we won't," insisted Sonic Boom and, with a wave of her wings, sent three eggs spinning out in front of the advancing trolls. They cracked as soon as they hit the metal floor, releasing a trio of impossibly cute baby griffins. The Grenade General gaped at the new arrivals.

"Awwwww," said one of the trolls. "How adorable."

"You're not wrong," said another. "Let's eat them."

The Grenade Generals lunged at the chicks who, in turn, lunged back. Before they knew what was happening, the trolls were yelping, trying to avoid the snapping beaks of Sonic's fierce infants. It was exactly the distraction the Skylanders needed. The heroes charged, fists flying, wrenches spinning, wings beating and fireballs flaming. A few seconds later, Sonic Boom's chicks had returned safely into their shells, Sprocket was tying up four unconscious trolls and Terrafin was handing out their pointed Grenade General helmets.

"It's not much of a disguise," Hot Dog commented as Terrafin plonked the helmet on the puppy's head.

"Yeah," agreed Sprocket. "Only an idiot would be fooled by these."

"Afternoon, Generals," saluted a passing Mace Major.

"Say no more," smiled Sonic Boom.

Wearing their stolen helmets, the Skylanders wheeled the trolley over to the doors and peered through their grimy windows.

"Woof woof, there he is!" yapped Hot Dog at the sight of Rocky, who was tied to a tiny chair in the middle of the room. A gag was wrapped around the Stone Golem's mouth and he was looking particularly sorry for himself.

"We need to get him outta there," Terrafin said, trying the doors, but they were locked.

"Allow me," said Sprocket, adjusting her goggles and igniting a laser cutter on the edge of her sleeve. Sparks flew as she sliced through the locking mechanism and the doors slid open.

"We must untie him," Sonic urged the others as they rushed towards the bound golem.

"Nm, mms m mmmp," murmured Rocky from behind the gag.

"Don't worry big guy," Terrafin said, already trying to untie the ropes that bound Rocky's arms together. "We'll have you out in no time."

"NM, MMS M MMMP!" Rocky repeated, sounding even more desperate.

"What's that?" asked Terrafin.

"Allow me," said Sonic Boom, snipping through Rocky's gag with her sharp beak.

"Thank you," the Stone Golem gasped, "but you should have listened to me."

"We couldn't understand you," explained

Terrafin. "What's the beef?"

"I was trying to tell you," Rocky explained, "it's a trap!"

"A trap?" Hot Dog repeated.

"Yes," came a voice from the doors. "A trap!"

The Skylanders spun round to see a large robot standing by the doors, hands on hips. Its paintwork was scored and blackened by a lifetime of standing too near to explosions. But that wasn't the strangest thing about the robot. No, the weirdest thing was that it had two heads.

"A trap you said was foolproof, Boom Two," said the left-hand head.

"It was foolproof, Boom One," said the right-hand head.

So these were the Boom Brothers: one robot with two heads.

"But you said it would catch the Skylanders, Boom Two," continued Boom One. "Not a bunch of treacherous trolls!"

"They're not trolls, you two-headed twit," said another, horribly familiar voice. "They're just wearing troll's helmets. Honestly, why am I surrounded by FOOOOOLS?"

The Boom Brothers wheeled out of the way to reveal a small bald figure in the doorway. A small bald figure who was grinning evilly at the Skylanders.

"Kaos," spat Terrafin, throwing off his disguise. "What are you up to?"

"Isn't it obvious, Terra-DIM?" the Portal Master screeched. "That grumpy golem is the

Earth segment of the Mask of Power. *My* Earth segment. There's nothing you can do to stop me, Sky-fools. Not this time."

"Wanna bet?" Terrafin snarled, his brass knuckles cracking in anticipation.

"Actually, yes," Kaos smirked. "Let's review the evidence. GLUMSHANKS!"

Kaos' butler appeared behind the Portal Master, carrying a clipboard.

"Yes, Lord Kaos?"

"Let's run through the checklist shall we? Capture the Earth segment?"

"Done!"

Kaos' awful smile grew wider.

"Trap the Skylanders in my Tricky Skylanders Trap of DOOOM?"

"Done!"

"Summon every troll in the factory as backup?"

Glumshanks looked over his shoulder to see the army of troll troops now jostling each other on the other side of the door.

"Done!" he concluded.

"So, there we have it! Still want that bet, Sharkbait?"

Terrafin thought about it for a minute. Kaos was right. The odds were against them. The situation was grim. There was no way they could win.

"Yeah, I bet you five dollars that you'll be laughing on the other side of your face by the end of the day . . . fool."

"WHAAAAAT?" screeched Kaos. "I call foolish fools fool, foolish fools never call me fool!"

"Get ready to pay up," snarled Terrafin, racing towards Kaos and drawing back a massive fist. "Easiest money I've ever made."

Kaos whimpered, pushed Glumshanks in front of him and screamed at the Boom Brothers. "The dynamite! Throw the dynamite now!"

Even as Terrafin swung a punch, the Boom Brothers reached into a drawer in their chest and pulled out what looked like a stick of dynamite. They lit the fuse, threw the glowing red stick under Terrafin's feet and went to shove their fingers in their ears – only to remember they were robots and didn't have any ears.

The dynamite detonated, but there was no flame or explosion. Just funky, groovy music.

"W-what's happening?" spluttered Terrafin as he began to dance.

"I don't know," replied Sonic Boom, her own paws jumping to the beat. "That sounds like Rocky."

"It is me," the Stone Golem whimpered. "They made me sing into their machine. I'm sorry."

The Boom Brothers threw more dynamite and the music got even louder. The Skylanders couldn't fight. They couldn't do anything other than dance.

"Bwa-ha-ha-ha-haaaaaaa," laughed Kaos, popping a pair of earplugs into his already wax-encrusted lug-holes. "My Disco Dynamite works. Bombs that make people dance so hard they'll be too exhausted to stop me."

"To stop you from doing what?" panted Hot Dog in the middle of his own hot-shoe shuffle.

"Taking over Skylands!" Kaos crowed. "What else, you DANCING FOOLS?"

CHAPTER TWELVE

TERRAFIN HAS AN IDEA

Terrafin had an idea. Gritting his teeth, he shimmied over to Hot Dog, pulling off a perfect salsa roll in the process. Meanwhile, the sizzling mutt had spun into a terrified tango, his feet no longer under the control of his doggy brain. Kaos was almost beside himself with laughter as the Boom Brothers lobbed more and more dynamite into the middle of the room. At this rate, the Skylanders would be dancing themselves into an early grave.

"Hot Dog," Terrafin bellowed. "When I give you the signal I want you to bark out a battery of flaming fireballs. Can you do that?"

Hot Dog nodded, his tongue lolling out of his mouth as he broke into a blistering bossa nova.

Terrafin hand-jived his way over to Sprocket, who was air-guitaring (with her spanner as the guitar).

"Sprocket, after Hot Dog's done his thing, you need to untie Rocky, you dig?"

"Got it," Sprocket replied, dropping to her knees and sliding across the floor.

Terrafin spun into a pirouette and leapt across to Sonic Boom like a knuckle-duster-wearing ballet dancer. There was just one more piece of his plan to put into place.

"Sonic Boom!" Terrafin shouted as the griffin began waltzing round and round in circles. "Screech, sister!"

"What?" Sonic yelled back, hardly able to hear him over Rocky's recorded voice.

"Screech!" Terrafin repeated, dropping into the splits and then twisting to spin on his head.

"Screech like you've never screeched before!"

A smile crept over Sonic's beak as she realized what Terrafin was asking. The Dirt Shark wished that he could stick his fingers in his ears, but instead he was forced into a rather impressive display of body popping. He gulped. He just hoped it wasn't his eardrums that popped next.

Sonic Boom opened her beak and screamed. "SCREEEEEEEEEEEEEEEEEEEEEEEEEEEE!!"

Terrafin had never heard anything like it. Sonic's cry was so loud that his teeth vibrated in his jaws, Sprocket's goggles shattered and Kaos' earplugs popped out of his ears like gold coins from Trigger Happy's gun.

The good news was that it also drowned out the sound of the Boom Brothers' Disco Dynamite.

The even better news was that they all stopped dancing.

The best news of all was that Terrafin's plan worked like the dreamiest dream that had ever been dreamed.

The moment the Disco Dynamite's spell was broken, Terrafin gave Hot Dog the thumbs up. The pup immediately barked out a wall of fireballs that fell perfectly at Kaos' feet, followed by another and another.

Now, the thing about metallic floors is that they conduct heat. Before long the floor beneath Kaos' feet were red-hot. No, white-hot. No, even hotter than that. With yelps that couldn't be heard above Sonic Boom's continuing screech, both the Portal Master and Glumshanks started hopping around from foot to steaming foot. Terrafin grinned – who was the dancing fool now, buster?

Behind him, Sprocket was untying Rocky as planned, but she had been spotted by the Boom Brothers. The two-headed robot lurched forward, arms outstretched, ready to stop her.

Oh no you don't, Terrafin thought. He leapt into the air and grabbed the metal siblings' heads in his huge hands. With a CLAAAANG

121

he slammed their heads together, sending their robotic eyes spinning in their cybernetic eye sockets. Stunned, the Boom Brothers veered around in a circle, stars dancing in front of their optic circuits, and bashed into Kaos and Glumshanks. The Portal Master and his sidekick were barged out through the doors and into the mass of trolls beyond, while the Boom Brothers toppled over, completely stunned.

Terrafin's plan had worked out even better than he'd hoped. The Dirt Shark darted forward as the doors hissed shut, and slammed his fist into the door controls. With a spark and a fizz the locking mechanism fused, sealing them in.

They were safe.

"Well done guys," Terrafin shouted, but no one could hear him. Sonic Boom was still screaming, her eyes shut tight with the effort. The Earth Skylander frowned. "OK, SB, you can shut it now!"

Sonic kept on screaming.

"I said, that's enough Sonic!" Terrafin bellowed.

More screams.

"THAT'S ENOUGH!"

His yelling finally got through. Sonic opened her eyes and shut her beak, a hurt look flashing over her face.

"OK," she sniffed. "There's no need to shout."

Terrafin broke into a toothy grin. "You did it, Sonic. You *all* did it. Well done guys."

"But what now?" barked Hot Dog. "We're stuck in here. Ruff!"

There was a thumping sound from the other side of the doors. The trolls were throwing explosives at the locks, hoping to blow them open.

"Oh no we're not," said Sprocket, peering at a bank of computers on the far wall. "You know how this place looks like a rocket?"

"What about it?" asked Terrafin.

"It *is* a rocket," Sprocket replied excitedly. "The biggest rocket I've ever seen. And that's not the best bit . . ."

She started pressing buttons and pulling levers, lost in the controls. The Skylanders looked at each other and rolled their eyes. Typical Sprocket. Give her a machine to play with and she'd forget you were even there.

"Care to share what the best bit is, then?" prompted Sonic.

"Hmmm?" Sprocket finally looked up. "Oh, sorry. This isn't just a room at the top of a tower that looks like a gigantic rocket because it actually *is* a gigantic rocket."

"It isn't?" yapped a slightly confused-looking Hot Dog.

"Nope. It's an escape capsule at the top of a tower that looks like a gigantic rocket because it actually is a gigantic rocket."

"So we can use it to –"

"Escape, yes," said Sprocket, going back to her controls. "The clue's in the name. I just need a little hush so I can prime the blasters. It's been a long time since they've . . ."

A muffled explosion covered the rest of her sentence.

"Those doors aren't going to last long," Rocky whimpered, turning to look at the windows as they slowly became criss-crossed with spider-webbing cracks.

But then, on the other side of the doors, the trolls parted, moving away.

"Hey hey hey," Hot Dog barked excitedly. "They're giving up. Losers!"

Terrafin shook his head. "They're not giving up. Look." He pointed at something that was being rolled down the corridor towards them.

"You're right," agreed Sonic, instinctively taking a step back. "They're just getting out of the way."

"Of what?" Sprocket asked absently from the mass of wires she had ripped out of the control panel.

"Of the biggest bomb you've ever seen," said Terrafin darkly.

CHAPTER THIRTEEN

THE ESCAPE POD

"**O**pen these doors, fools," Kaos screamed through the glass. "Or be blown to KINGDOM COOOOME!"

"Can you work any quicker, Sprocket?" Terrafin asked, ignoring the evil Portal Master but never taking his eyes off the very round and very large bomb. "As in, can you get us out of here right now?"

Sprocket shook her head.

"I'm going as fast as I can," she said with a mouth full of wires. "It'll take as long as it takes."

Behind the doors, Kaos was tapping his foot impatiently.

"Last chance, SKYLOSERS. Are you coming out or not?"

"Not!" barked back Hot Dog.

"Riiiiiiight," screeched Kaos. "Light the fuse of the Extra Explosive Bomb of Explosive EXPLOSION!"

Immediately, every troll in the corridor started patting down their armour.

Kaos let his head fall into his hands. "Please tell me someone has a match?"

There was more frantic checking of armoured pockets, before a weedy voice was heard from the back of the throng.

"I have, Lord Kaos! I have!"

A small troll rushed forward, a huge oversized match held proudly above his pointed ears.

"Then light it," Kaos crowed, grinning evilly through the glass. "Light the most bomby bomb in the history of BOOOOMBS!"

Terrafin had to think fast. There was no way the doors could withstand the force of such a large explosive. His eyes darted around the room until they came to rest on a microphone on the console next to Sprocket. That was it. The intercom the Boom Brothers had used to communicate with the rest of the factory.

The Dirt Shark rushed over to the mic, grabbing Rocky.

"Time for another solo, song boy," he said, switching the microphone on. A squeal of feedback echoed round the room. "Sing like yo' life depends on it – which it sorta does."

"But if I sing you'll be helpless," Rocky said sadly.

"Don't worry about that," Sprocket said, looking up from her work to swing her spanner into the next bank of computers. Buttons shot everywhere from the smashed controls. "Instant ear-plugs. Stick 'em in."

The Skylanders did as they were told and, with a shrug, Rocky started to sing. Terrafin spun around, biting his bottom lip (which is always a risky thing for a shark to do).

Rocky's song belted from every speaker in the factory but the troll had already lit the match and was lifting it to the fuse. Were they too late?

The match swung up to the end of the fuse and . . .

. . . the troll started tapping his toes.

The tapping turned into a shuffle and the shuffle turned into a jig and the jig turned into a prance and the prance turned into a full-on boogie.

The match dropped to the floor and was extinguished under the dancing feet of the troll army.

Meanwhile, the oversized bomb started to roll back, straight over Kaos.

"Waaaaaaaaah!" hollered the rotten Portal Master as he disappeared from view.

"Way to go," Terrafin whooped, punching the air in triumph. "Now, what are you waiting for, Sprocket? Let's blow this joint."

His face fell as he turned to face the Golding. The Tech Skylander wasn't working on the controls. She was pointing to where Hot Dog had been standing seconds before. Now, the puppy was held fast by a metal hand. A metal hand that belonged to the Boom Brothers.

"Forgotten about us?" gloated Boom One, the robots' other hand tucked behind their back.

"Thought we were scrap?" sneered Boom Two.

"Big mistake," concluded Boom One.

"Biggest ever," added Boom Two.

Hot Dog wriggled in their grasp but was held tight.

"Don't worry about me," he barked. "Just – ruff – get us out of here."

Terrafin glanced at Sprocket. She had finished her work and the escape pod was ready to fire. All she needed to do was hit the big red button on the control console.

Terrafin was about to tell her to push it, when Sonic Boom stepped forward. "Wait," she warned, through clenched teeth. "We don't know what they've got in their other hand."

The Boom Brothers grinned in unison. It was an evil, oily grin.

"Not as stupid as you look, are you?" said Boom One.

"No one could be as stupid as they look," said Boom Two, drawing their hand from behind their back.

Sonic gasped, not quite believing what she was seeing.

"That's right," snarled Boom One, holding up a large piece of yellow fruit. A large piece of yellow *ticking* fruit. "We've got a pineapple grenade."

"And we're not afraid to use it," added Boom Two. "Surrender or this entire room goes boom."

CHAPTER FOURTEEN

BOW BEFORE THE BOOM BROTHERS

"Surrender?" Sprocket laughed. "You don't know who you're dealing with."

"Skylanders never surrender," Sonic Boom snarled, moving alongside her gleaming teammate. "Never, ever give in."

"And don't you forget it," added Hot Dog, never taking his eyes from the explosive fruit. "Right, Terrafin?"

"Hey, let's not be too hasty here, hot shot," Terrafin said, raising his hands. "Maybe surrendering isn't such a bad idea."

"What?" gasped Sprocket, not quite believing

her ears. "You're joking?"

The Dirt Shark shook his head.

"'Fraid not, Sprock," he shrugged, letting his hands fall down to his sides in defeat. "This is one Skylander who knows when he's beat."

"But . . ." Sonic began, then realized she didn't know what to say, so decided to just say "but" again for good measure.

"I mean it, Sonic," Terrafin admitted. "I faced some pretty mean opponents in the past, but nothing like these guys. They make Kaos look like a featherweight. They're the real deal."

"Finally," screamed Boom One, metallic chest swelling with pride, "someone who recognizes our genius, brother."

"I know," sniffed Boom Two, an oily tear slipping down his burnished cheek. "I'm getting quite emotional."

"It's over guys," said Terrafin, sinking down to his knees. "Bow before the Boom Brothers."

The other Skylanders were so shocked that

they found themselves doing the same, kneeling in front of the robot. Hot Dog whimpered in bewilderment.

"You might as well stop singing as well, Rock," Terrafin said sadly. "It's over."

The Stone Golem fell silent, not knowing what to say. Behind them the trolls all stopped dancing and the Skylanders could hear the muffled voice of Kaos demanding that they get the Extra Explosive Bomb of Explosive Explosion off him at once.

"I do just have one question," piped up Terrafin, raising his nose to face the brothers.

"Yes?" asked Boom One, intrigued.

"What do you want to know?" asked Boom Two.

A smile played on Terrafin's thin lips.

"Who comes up with all the ideas for your amazing bombs?"

"That's simple," said Boom One. "It's me."

"You liar," spluttered Boom Two. "They're all

my ideas."

"Don't be stupid," retaliated Boom One. "I'm the brains in this family."

"No, you're not."

"Am too."

"Are not."

"Am too."

Terrafin's smile had spread into a grin. As the Boom Brothers were lost in their argument, he indicated for the others to cover their heads with their hands.

"So, I suppose you think this pineapple grenade was all your own work?" screamed Boom One.

"Well it wasn't yours, you clog-headed numbskull," came back Boom Two. "You couldn't blow up a paper bag, let alone an explosive device."

"I've never been so insulted in all my days," hissed Boom One. "Take that back, you pathetic excuse for a piston engine."

"Shan't," snapped Boom Two. "The day you invent a half-decent detonator is the day I eat my hat."

"Eat your hat?" screamed Boom One. "Eat this!"

And with that Boom One shoved the pineapple grenade into Boom Two's open mouth. The second head gagged, releasing Hot Dog who leapt nimbly back to the other Skylanders. Gagging, Boom Two swallowed the explosive fruit, which clanged down into the robots' metallic stomach.

The Boom Brothers' jaws gaped at each other as they realized what they had done before turning to face Terrafin, whose grin had never been wider.

"You do realize this is your fault?" whimpered Boom One as the grenade stopped ticking.

"No, it was . . ."

BOOOOOOOOOOOOOM!

The Boom Brothers exploded in a hail of metal parts.

As the smoke cleared, the Skylanders began to laugh, realizing what Terrafin had been doing all along.

"You knew they would argue," Sonic Boom said, brushing cogs from her feathers.

"It was all a trick," said Sprocket, pushing red hair out of her eyes.

"Of course it was," barked Hot Dog, giving Terrafin a sizzling lick. "He's the champ. He'd never let us down. Woof!"

"All very touching," came a voice from the other side of the doors, "but I think you're forgetting something. KAOOOOOS!!"

Terrafin turned to see Kaos glaring through the window, another match in his hand.

"You won't defeat me as easily as those bickering bucket-heads," Kaos snarled. "Now open these doors and give me my Earth segment or I'll blow you into even smaller pieces than the Boom Brothers."

Terrafin smiled. "No problem. Sprocket, why

don't you hit that big red button and open the doors?"

Kaos smirked the smirkiest smirk in history.

"You mean this big red button here?" Sprocket asked, moving over to the console.

"That's the one."

"Consider it done." Sprocket slammed her open palm down on the button. "Oh, hang on," she said, trying hard to suppress a giggle. "That's not the door control."

A look of mock panic crossed Terrafin's face. "You're right. That was the button that launches the rockets. I must be punch drunk!"

The room began to shake. In fact, the entire tower began to shake. On the other side of the door, Kaos started choking on the thick acrid smoke that was billowing around him as the escape pod rockets fired.

"Hold on to something," Sprocket shouted. "Take off in five seconds. Maybe even two."

"You haven't heard the last of this,

Skylanders!" Kaos raged from the other side of the doors. "I, Kaos, will find the next segment, whatever happens. And then, you shall all be DOOOOMED!"

"Whatever, Kaos," Terrafin smiled, bracing himself for take off. "Just remember one thing."

"What's that, fool?"

"You owe me five dollars."

The rockets fired and the escape pod shot into the air, high above the Junk Mountains. Beneath them, the Boom Brothers' Explosive Emporium collapsed into a heap, trapping Kaos and the troll army inside.

CHAPTER FIFTEEN

THE EARTH SEGMENT

"**D**o you think Kaos got away?" Sonic Boom asked as they walked through the gardens of the Eternal Archives.

"Reckon so," Terrafin rumbled. "That cat's got more lives than a . . . well, you know."

"At least we got Rocky away safely," Sprocket said, swinging her spanner over her shoulder.

"And blasted home in time for tea," Hot Dog yapped happily.

"Although I'll be happy if I never set foot in another escape capsule again," admitted Terrafin. "That was no way to travel."

In front of them, Master Eon turned at the sound of Terrafin's voice.

"Ah, just in time," the Portal Master said. "Young Rocky is going to sing for us."

"Then I hope you've got your dancing shoes on, Master," Terrafin laughed, imagining the aged Portal Master cutting a rug.

"That won't be necessary this time, Terrafin. Watch."

At a nod from Eon, the Stone Golem cleared his throat and began to sing, the same note-perfect tune as before – but this time it *was* different. Eon raised his hand and light blared from Rocky's mouth. The Skylanders shielded their eyes, but when the glare faded, the song had finished. Terrafin looked up and gasped. There, spinning in the air, was the Earth segment of the Mask of Power.

"But I thought Rocky *was* the segment."

Eon shook his head as the fragment floated magically down into his open palm.

"No, only his singing voice. A light, enchanted tune – the complete opposite to heavy, stony Earth."

"I was given my singing voice centuries ago," Rocky admitted, "when I was only a rock-tot. Before then I couldn't sing a note."

"By a Spell Punk, I'd wager," said Eon, tucking the segment safely in his robes. "One of the mages who split the Mask of Power in the first place."

"But will Rocky still be able to sing?" Sonic Boom asked, looking up at the Portal Master.

Eon shook his head sadly. "I'm afraid not. His amazing gift has been lost forever."

Terrafin gave the Stone Golem a friendly punch in the arm. Rocky flinched a little, but then smiled at his new friend.

"Hey, sorry about that big fella. What you goin' to do?"

"Oh, I've got a few ideas," said Rocky, his stony smile slowly turning into a wide grin.

With a flash, they were back at Professor Puck's Fantastic Fairy Fair.

"I don't get it," admitted Terrafin as they leapt from the Portal. "Why d'ya wanna come back to this dump?"

"I think I know why," said Sonic Boom, sharing a secret smile with Rocky.

"There you are," boomed a voice from behind. "My number one star. You came back to me!"

The Skylanders turned to see Professor Puck rushing towards them, his moustache bristling with pleasure.

"Hello Professor. Sorry I'm late."

"Don't worry about that, dear boy," the untrustworthy gnome snapped. "You've got work to do. The audience is waiting for your comeback performance. We've sold more tickets than ever before. Come on, come on."

And with that, Professor Puck bustled Rocky

across to his tent.

"He didn't even say thank you," muttered Sprocket.

"Yeah, that's ruff," barked Hot Dog.

"I wouldn't be so sure," said Sonic Boom enigmatically. "I think the Professor is about to get everything he deserves.

Terrafin's eyes glinted as he got Sonic's meaning. "Come on," he laughed, sprinting towards the tent. "I do not want to miss this."

"Ladies and gentlemen," announced Professor Puck as Rocky shuffled onto the stage of the big tent. "This is the moment you've been waiting for. The sensational, the spectacular, the songtastic, ROCKY!"

"But – woof woof – Rocky can't sing any more," yapped Hot Dog, bewildered.

"I think that's the point," Terrafin sniggered. "Cover your ears."

"But his power's gone too," Sprocket pointed

out. "We won't dance this time."

"That's not what Terrafin means," explained Sonic Boom, placing her paws over her ears.

On the stage, Rocky opened his mouth and began to sing.

It was the worst noise you'd ever heard, like two boulders grinding together. Rocky sounded like someone gargling with gravel.

"What a racket," one of the crowd shouted out.

"I thought you said he could sing," yelled another.

"It's a swizz," came another cry. "Professor Puck tried to con us!"

On the stage, Professor Puck's bushy moustache drooped as he tried to calm the jeering crowd.

"Now, let's not be too hasty, my friends. This is all just a big misunderstanding."

"Boo!" A squashy tomato flew from the crowd, only narrowly missing the panicking Puck.

"It's a con!" Another tomato.

"I want my money back!" Puck dodged a rotten egg.

"Run him out of town!" The Professor turned and fled.

The crowd tore after the fleeing fairground owner, chasing him off into the distance.

"Oh dear," Sonic Boom said, as she watched them go. "I think the Professor's reputation is in tatters."

"Ah well," grinned Sprocket. "Fair's fair."

"I think you've just performed your last gig," Terrafin told Rocky as he clambered down from the stage. The golem smiled, displaying a huge row of shiny stones where most of us have teeth.

"That's music to my ears, Terrafin," said Rocky. "Music to my ears!"

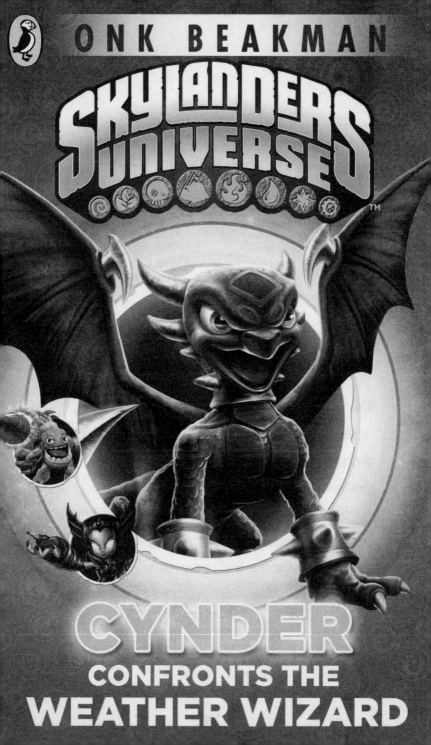

CHAPTER ONE

THE ONCOMING STORM

"**O**h yeah," said Zook, reaching for another coconut drink. "This is the life, right Cynder?"

Beside the Bambazooker, the dark purple dragon shifted uncomfortably beneath the shade of a large parasol.

"Speak for yourself, bamboo boy," she sighed. "Remind me again why we're lying on a beach?"

"To soak up the sun, why else?" The green-barked Life Skylander slurped the creamy coconut milk noisily. "This is the Cloudless Desert, the sunniest spot in all of Skylands. Just kick back and relax, that's all."

"And you don't feel guilty that we're wasting our time when we should be out looking for the next segment of the Mask of Power?" Cynder snapped, her scaly brow furrowing. She glanced around, taking in the countless Mabu, Molekin and even the odd cyclops that were out enjoying a day in the sun. Didn't they realize the danger they were all in? Kaos was trying to reassemble the fabled Mask of Power. If he managed it . . .

"Hey, hey, hey, just chill," insisted Zook, settling back in his deckchair. "If Master Eon needs us, he knows where to find us."

The buzz of the happy holidaymakers was broken by a sharp crack that sounded like the universe being pulled in two. Cynder was immediately on her feet. She knew that sound. It was a Portal!

She spun round to see a column of light blaze into existence, a figure materializing at its heart. Tall, regal and strangely unnerving.

Cynder grinned. Zook wanted to chill and you couldn't get more chilling than this new arrival. Hex!

The elven sorceress swept from the Portal, her piercing gaze passing over the beach. All around, there were gasps and even a few whimpers. Like Cynder, Hex was an Undead Skylander, but a mistress of dark magic and feared by many. Hex's ghost-white eyes shimmered as she watched the holidaymakers frantically pack up their towels and windbreaks, deciding that there was something else they'd rather be doing. Like getting trapped in a spider-infested cave or fed to a pack of zombies.

"What's up, Hexy?" called Zook in greeting. "You here to catch the rays?" The Bambazooker peeked over his pair of ridiculously large sunglasses. "You do look like you could do with a tan."

Hex's narrow mouth turned down at the corners. She wasn't known for her sense of humour. She was known for striking fear into everyone's hearts, which was quite different.

"Master Eon needs you," she replied, her

voice like wind whistling through a graveyard. "You'll have to 'catch your rays' another time." Her disgust at the very concept was obvious. Hex was more at home in moonlight than in the warmth of the sun.

"Is it the Mask?" Cynder said eagerly, feeling an electric thrill run through her wings. "Has Eon located the next segment?"

But Hex didn't answer. Instead she was peering into the sky, a puzzled look on her ashen face.

"I thought this place was known as the Cloudless Desert?" she commented, floating up from the blisteringly hot sands.

"Yeah, that's right," Zook confirmed contentedly. "Not a cloud in the sky."

"Except that one," Hex muttered, cocking her head to the side in curiosity.

Cynder followed her gaze. The witch was right. A tiny cloud had appeared in the expanse of brilliant blue. A cloud that was growing, and growing fast. A shadow fell over the sands as the three Skylanders gazed up in amazement. In a matter of seconds the cloud had smothered the sky, becoming darker with every passing minute.

"Hey, who turned off the sun?" complained Zook, throwing aside his shades and snatching up his bazooka. Fun-loving and carefree he may be, but Zook recognized a threat when he saw one.

So did Cynder. Her expression was darkening as quickly as the sky. This was no natural storm.

"It is the power of Darkness," cried Hex, throwing her arms out wide, crackling phantom orbs appearing in her upturned palms. "The forces of nature have turned against us."

Cynder felt a drop of rain on her nose, followed by another. A moment later, the heavens opened, water lashing down from those strange storm clouds.

"It could just be a quick shower," joked Zook, ever the eternal optimist. "I mean, who ever got hurt by a few drops of rain?"

There was a scream from their left. The

Skylanders turned to see a Mabu sinking into the sodden sand. He was already up to his waist in the quagmire. All around, fleeing holidaymakers were getting stuck, before being dragged beneath the dunes.

Even Cynder could feel the grip of the wet ground pulling her claws down into a clammy embrace.

"We need to do something," she yelled, flapping her leathery wings to pull herself free with a wet plop. "The dunes are turning into quicksand. Everyone is going to be sucked underground!"

Can Cynder save the stricken sun-worshippers? What evil is lurking on Undead Isle? And can a Skylander really turn bad?

Find out all this and more in . . .

CYNDER
CONFRONTS THE
WEATHER WIZARD

Which Skylander is your favourite - the boxing Dirt Shark or the loud-mouthed mother-griffin?

TERRAFIN

ROUND 1: ORIGINS

This shark-of-all-trades has done it all, from Dirt Seas lifeguard to brawny boxing champ. But he didn't find his true calling until Master Eon spotted his heroic potential and offered him a choice: continue defending his title, or save the world as a Skylander. It was no contest!

ROUND 2: BATTLE CRY

It's Feeding Time!

ROUND 3: PERSONALITY

Terrafin may be a little rough and ready, but he's always ready to use his mighty shark-fists to protect the innocent.

ROUND 4: WEAPONS

Quick on his feet, Terrafin is even quicker underground. He burrows through the earth and bursts up to deliver his signature blow – a big bellyflop!

ROUND 5: SPECIAL ABILITIES

When the going gets tough, the tough launch frenzied mini-sharks to swarm all over the enemy. Oh yeah!

TOTAL:

Give each category a rating out of 10, then add them all up. Whoever receives the highest score is your favourite!

SONIC BOOM

ROUND 1: ORIGINS

Thanks to the curse of an evil sorcerer, Sonic Boom's offspring are trapped in a circle of eternal re-birth. But it's not all bad news for the caring griffin mother, for she's trained her hatchlings to crack some serious shell. Now, they head into battle together as an entire family of Skylanders.

ROUND 2: BATTLE CRY

Full Scream Ahead!

ROUND 3: PERSONALITY

Cunning and brave, Sonic Boom hates bullies and her maternal instincts extend beyond her clutch of cursed eggs.

ROUND 4: WEAPONS

Cover your ears. Sonic Boom's Sonic Roar will do more than give you a headache. It can send you flying. And if that cry doesn't get you, her babies will!

ROUND 5: SPECIAL ABILITIES

When one chick is better than three, Sonic Boom can cast a spell that combines her babies into a super sprog.

TOTAL: